PARENTS AND CAREGIVERS,

Stone Arch Readers are designed to provide enjoyable reading experiences, as well as opportunities to develop vocabulary, literacy skills, and comprehension. Here are a few ways to support your beginning reader:

* Talk with your child about the ideas addressed in the story.

* Discuss each illustration, mentioning the characters, where they are, and what they are doing.

* Read with expression, pointing to each word. You may want to read the whole story through and then revisit parts of the story to ensure that the meanings of words or phrases are understood.

* Talk about why the character did what he or she did and what your child would do in that situation.

* Help your child connect with characters and events in the story.

Remember, reading with your child should be fun, not forced. Each moment spent reading with your child is a priceless investment in his or her literacy life.

GAIL SAUNDERS-SMITH, PH.D.

STONE ARCH **READERS**

are published by Stone Arch Books
A Capstone Imprint
151 Good Counsel Drive, P.O. Box 669, Mankato, Minnesota 56002
www.capstonepub.com

Library of Congress Cataloging-in-Publication data
is available on the Library of Congress website.

Summary: Moopy's day at the beach
is almost ruined by Ora's digging.

Library Binding: 978-1-4342-1874-2
Paperback: 978-1-4342-2304-3

Creative Director: Heather Kindseth
Designer: Bob Lentz
Production Specialist: Michelle Biedscheid

Reading Consultants:
Gail Saunders-Smith, Ph.D.
Melinda Melton Crow, M.Ed.
Laurie K. Holland, Media Specialist

MOOPY
ON THE
BEACH

BY CARI MEISTER

ILLUSTRATED BY
DENNIS MESSNER

STONE ARCH BOOKS
a capstone imprint

snacks

MOOPY

This is Moopy. She lives underground. She likes it there.

There are tasty bugs to eat. There are fun dance clubs.

There is space for digging.
Moopy is a great digger. Look at
her claws!

But, sometimes, Moopy likes
to go up.

It smells different.

There are different things
to eat.

And there is the sun! Moopy
loves the sun! It feels so good on
her skin.

Today, Moopy is at the beach.

"I love the sound of waves," she says.

"I love the smell of salt," she says.

Moopy lies down on her towel. She digs her claws into the sand.

"Ah!" she says. "This is perfect."

It is not perfect for long.

Buzz! Clank, clank, clink.

"What is that?" asks Moopy.

She sticks her nose in the air.
Sniff, sniff.

"Oh no!" she says. "Another
monster!"

"Hello!" says the monster.
"My name is Ora. I am looking
for gold. This is my new gold
finder. Do you want to see how
it works?"

Moopy does not care about gold finders. Moopy does not want to be bothered.

She flips over on her towel.

"What a rude monster!" says Ora.

Click, clank, buzz.

Ora walks on the beach with her gold finder.

Click, click, click.

The gold is under Moopy!

"Please go away," says Moopy.

"There is gold under you!" says Ora.

"I do not care," says Moopy. "Look somewhere else."

Soon, Moopy falls asleep in the sun.

"Her snores are loud," says Ora. "She won't even hear me digging."

Ora gets out her shovel. She starts to dig.

Ora is excited. She digs very fast.

Oh no! Ora is getting sand all over Moopy!

Moopy wakes up.

"What are you doing?" she yells. "You got sand on my towel. You got sand on my legs. You even got sand up my nose!"

"I am sorry," says Ora.
"But you will not get any more
sand on you if you move from
that spot."

Moopy does not move.

"This is my spot," she says.

"Please," says Ora. "I have
not found gold in weeks! I need
it to finish my gold dance floor."

Moopy stands up. "You like to dance?" asks Moopy.

"Yes!" says Ora. "I like to polka. I like to waltz. I like to rumba best."

Moopy pictures herself
dancing on a gold dance floor.

"If I help dig," asks Moopy, "can I dance on your golden floor?"

"Of course!" says Ora.

The two of them start to dig.

"Gold!" says Ora.

A week later, Ora keeps her promise. She invites Moopy to try out the new dance floor.

"You are a good digger," says
Ora.

"But you are an even better dancer!" she says.

THE END

STORY WORDS

underground   snores   rumba

towel   excited   invites

perfect   polka

sniff   waltz

Total Word Count: 448

READ MORE MONSTER STORIES!